Pete & Penny Penguin LEARN
COMMON CENTS

Written and Illustrated by Caitlyn Stupi

To Mom and Dad,
Thank you for everything, always.
With all my love,
Your Little Penguin

Meet Pete and Penny Penguin! During the winter,
they would travel to their grandparents' igloo.
They loved spending time with Granny and Papa!

Besides creating lots of fun memories, Pete and
Penny would always learn an important lesson, too!

Sliding in the snow, Pete and Penny raced along and
chatted about all the fun things they've done on past visits -
from helping around the igloo to playing new games.

When Pete and Penny arrived, they celebrated with homemade snow cones and swam around the iceberg.

Granny and Papa told them about all the activities they had planned, but it was time to head inside for dinner.
Pete and Penny couldn't wait to have some of Granny's fishcakes!

It was a perfect day.

Later that evening after a big dinner, Granny wanted to teach the kids how to knit hats and scarves. Pete fell fast asleep, but Penny paid close attention. She was fascinated by the way Granny could make something out of just a ball of yarn.

Granny explained she liked knitting because she could sell her crafts to earn money or give them to others in need. Penny thought this was very wise and kind of Granny.

The next day, Granny gave Pete and Penny small jobs so they could earn some money before their trip to the market. The kids took a birthday balloon to a neighbor, mopped the floors, and helped at a yard sale.

Granny knew it was important for the kids to learn that earning must come before spending!

When their work was finished, Granny paid Pete and Penny, thanking them for a job well done. The kids were so excited to have their own spending money, so they wanted to go to the market right away!

Papa gave the kids permission to go shopping since Granny
was busy knitting. Whenever Pete and Penny had money, they
liked to spend it right away.

They rushed to the market and spent all of their money on hot
cocoa and some small toys. They still wanted to get some fish
pops, but they were out of money!

Where did all the money go so quickly?

Pete and Penny went back to the igloo and searched for more money. They found Papa's change jar and figured it would be okay to take what they needed without asking.

Papa saw them taking the change. He was a bit confused because they had just earned money for doing chores. He could only guess that Granny had given them permission.

Papa checked with Granny to see if she knew that the kids were taking from the change jar. Granny was shocked as Pete and Penny were just paid for their morning chores.

Why would they be taking without asking?
What happened to all their earnings?
Why did they need more money?

Granny gave it some thought and realized Pete and Penny needed a lesson about money.

Granny and Papa explained to Pete and Penny that it was important to save some of their earnings for future purchases, or even to help others. If they kept spending it as soon as they earned it, they would always feel like they needed more – and taking money without asking is not okay.

Pete and Penny were sent back into town with some money and instructions to purchase milk and bread. Granny and Papa gave them permission to keep two dollars from the change to put into their savings.

Pete and Penny were excited to go back into the market because they saw so many things they liked!

While at the market, they were overcome with excitement!

Instead of purchasing bread and milk,
they spent all of the money - including the money for
their savings - on fish popsicles and a toy boat.

Pete and Penny realized on the way home that not only did they spend the money irresponsibly - they even spent their savings!

When they got back to the igloo, Papa was very frustrated with their unwise spending. Something had to be done to help them understand how money really works!

Papa explained that money comes from hard work
and that they should be responsible with their earnings.

Granny explained that there is a difference between wants
and needs. While Pete and Penny wanted their treats, they
needed the milk and bread.

Because Pete and Penny were now responsible for buying the missing milk and bread with their own money, they had to come up with a plan.

So, they began earning money by doing chores around the Igloo and opening a snow cone stand in the neighborhood.

They also earned money by giving sledding tours
and selling their knitted crafts at the market.

After days of working hard, Papa and Granny could see
the kids thinking about how challenging earning, spending
and saving could be.

Granny told Papa that she thought it was time
to teach the kids "Common Cents" – a way she learned
to manage money when she was a little penguin!

Granny explained the "Common Cents" plan to the kids.
Pete and Penny each got three piggy banks marked
"Save" "Spend" and "Give."

She taught them that when money is earned, some should go
into each bank. They should remember to spend it carefully,
save it often, and give it to help others.

Granny asked if Pete or Penny could think of
ways to spend carefully.

The kids have always wanted ice skates, but could never afford them. Penny suggested instead of them each purchasing a pair of ice skates, they could just buy one pair and take turns.

Pete realized this would allow them to have money to put into savings at the Snow Town Bank! They could eventually save for a second pair of ice skates or have money for a future purchase.

Finally, Granny asked the kids to think of someone they could help who doesn't have much money.

Pete and Penny suggested using some of their money to help fix Polar Bear Patty's broken sled.

Pete and Penny became more excited about saving, spending, and giving. It wasn't as hard as they thought! It even inspired them to think about ways of earning money when they grow up.

Pete said in the future he'd like to earn money by owning his own market. Penny said one day, she would like to earn money by working at Snow Town Bank.

Granny and Papa were very proud of Pete and Penny Penguin.

Not only did they learn that there are many ways to earn money,
but they also learned the "Common Cents" plan of
spending, saving, and giving!

When Pete and Penny returned home, they told their parents
about the many ways they were able to earn money and
how important it is to think before spending.

They shared that saving is also important because it allows for
future spending and giving to others who need help.

Finally, Pete and Penny shared that because Granny and Papa
taught them earning, spending, and saving is possible for anyone,
they now dream of having rewarding jobs of their own one day.

A Note to Educators and Caregivers

Thank you for taking an interest in teaching the next generation the importance of personal finances. Financial literacy has become an educational priority due to its link to personal wellbeing. Research indicates that when young children are introduced to the concept of earning money and having jobs, it fuels their curiosity about career choices and opens their eyes to the many possibilities in store for their futures. After enjoying Pete and Penny's story, we hope you will continue the conversation about personal finances with the following discussion and reinforcement questions.

What talent or skill did Granny use to earn money? Can you think of a skill you'd like to learn in order to perform a job? Do you have a talent you could use to earn money?

Earning money allows us to pay for food and clothes or to purchase toys, but can you think of something else kind that you can do with the money you earn?

Have you ever been paid to do a job or help with a task? What did you do with the money?

When Pete and Penny earned money, they rushed to the market to spend it right away. Was this smart spending? Why? What is the difference between wants and needs?

Do you think it was okay for Pete and Penny to take Papa's money from the change jar without asking?

Granny told Pete and Penny about the "Common Cents" plan using three piggy banks, what was written on each bank?

Why is saving important? Can you think of things that you or your family might need to save for?

Meet the Author & Artist

Designer and illustrator, Caitlyn Stupi, brings to life art that educates in "Pete and Penny Penguin Learn Common Cents." A native Marylander, artist, dancer, cellist and life-long lover of penguins, Caitlyn chose Pete and Penny to be the ambassadors for her social impact initiative, Common Cents. Common Cents is a financial literacy awareness campaign targeted towards primary grade level students to help them understand the basics of personal finances and foster more secure futures. Research shows that when children are introduced to the concept of earning, it fuels their vision for career aspirations. Caitlyn is passionate about empowering youth, regardless of their socioeconomic status, gender, or race, to set goals and chase their dreams.

CPSIA information can be obtained
at www.ICGtesting.com
Printed in the USA
LVHW051913161219
640672LV00011B/499